SHY
CHARLES

170201

ROSEMARY WELLS

Viking

VIKING
Published by the Penguin Group
Penguin Putnam Books for Young Readers,
345 Hudson Street, New York, New York 10014, U.S.A.
Penguin Books Ltd, 27 Wrights Lane, London W8 5TZ, England
Penguin Books Australia Ltd, Ringwood, Victoria, Australia
Penguin Books Canada Ltd, 10 Alcorn Avenue, Toronto, Ontario, Canada M4V 3B2
Penguin Books (N.Z.) Ltd, 182-190 Wairau Road, Auckland 10, New Zealand

Penguin Books Ltd, Registered Offices: Harmondsworth, Middlesex, England

First published in 1988 by Dial, a division of Penguin Books USA Inc.
Published in 2001 by Viking, a division of Penguin Putnam Books for Young Readers

1 3 5 7 9 10 8 6 4 2

The Library of Congress has catalogued the Dial edition as follows:
Wells, Rosemary / Shy Charles.
Summary / Being painfully timid and shy does not keep a young mouse from
rescuing his baby-sitter in an emergency situation.
[1. Mice—Fiction. 2. Bashfulness—Fiction
3. Baby-sisters—Fiction. 4. Stories in rhyme.]
I. Title.
PZ8.3.W465Sh 1988 [E] 87-27247
ISBN 0-8037-0563-8
ISBN 0-8037-0564-6 (lib. bdg)

Viking ISBN 0-670-88729-3

The art for each picture consists of a black ink and watercolor painting,
which is camera-separated and reproduced in full color.

Printed in Hong Kong
Set in Minister

For shy Victoria

Charles was happy as he could be,

But he liked to play alone.
He wouldn't talk to Wanda Sue,

And he never went near the phone.

"It's a new day," said Charles's mother.
"Let's go in the store and say hello.
We'll buy a sweet-potato pie.
And we'll say good-bye before we go."

"Wonderful morning!" said Mrs. Belinski.
"A chocolate surprise for my beautiful boy!"

"Say thank you," whispered Charles's mother.
"Thank you!" yelled Mrs. Belinski. "Enjoy!"

His mother told him, "Say good-bye!"
Charles hid inside a flour sack.
"Good-bye with kisses," said Mrs. Belinksi.
"Someday when he's big, he'll kiss me back!"

"I'm so embarrassed," said Charles's mother.
"You never say good-bye or thank you.
Lucky for you that I'm so nice.
Another mother would spank you!"

"This can't go on," said Charles's dad.
"I'm sick and tired of thank-you fights.
It's time he played football or joined the ballet."

Next Tuesday Charles was in tights.

"Isn't he sweet!" cried Madame LaFleur.
Charles wouldn't say maybe or no or yes.

For a week he pretended to be asleep.

Charles was not a success.

So Charles's father took him to town
And bought him some beautiful football things.
The shirt was scarlet with shoulder pads.
The helmet had silver wings.

"Charles," said his father, "you'll be the best!
Like lightning you'll streak across the grass.
Like butter you'll melt the defensive line.
And you'll throw the winning pass!"

Charles trembled like an autumn leaf.
"Hi!" roared the coach, "my name is Fred.

"He doesn't look so well to me.
Take him home and put him to bed."

"Charles!" said his dad. "You're a jelly roll!
You're just a cowardly custard.
/ˈkaʊədli/   /ˈkʌstəd/
You're like a sandwich without the bread
Not to mention the ham and mustard.
How will you ever go to school
or find a job or get married?"
Charles sat down and cried so hard . . .

He had to be carried.

Then Charles's father murmured low,
"A baby-sitter is coming tonight.
You know the one. It's Mrs. Block.
And everything will be all right."

The sun went down. The sitter came.
His parents left at six o'clock.

Charles skedaddled up the stairs.
"Come back, little pushcake!" cried Mrs. Block.

Charles played happily in his room.
He made a spaceship out of his chairs.
Suddenly there was a terrible crash . . .

Mrs. Block had fallen downstairs.

Charles got her onto the sofa.
He told her, "Now, don't be nervous!"

He brought her a blanket and cocoa,
Then he called the emergency service.

"He saved my life," moaned Mrs. Block.
"He's a prince, a gem, a hero!"

And everyone shouted, "Thank you, Charles!"
But Charles said . . .

Zero.